An I Can Read Book™

S0-BRF-753

Last One In
is a
ROTTEN EGG

Leonard Kessler

HarperTrophy®
A Division of HarperCollinsPublishers

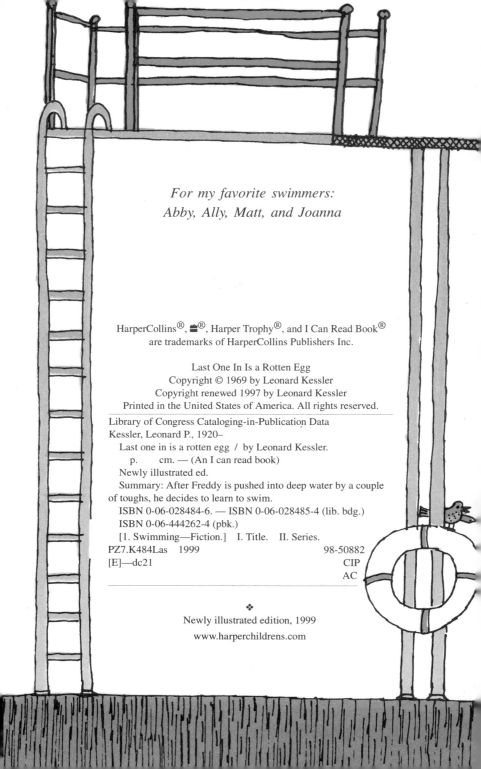

For my favorite swimmers:
Abby, Ally, Matt, and Joanna

HarperCollins®, 📖®, Harper Trophy®, and I Can Read Book®
are trademarks of HarperCollins Publishers Inc.

Last One In Is a Rotten Egg
Copyright © 1969 by Leonard Kessler
Copyright renewed 1997 by Leonard Kessler
Printed in the United States of America. All rights reserved.

Library of Congress Cataloging-in-Publication Data
Kessler, Leonard P., 1920–
    Last one in is a rotten egg / by Leonard Kessler.
        p.   cm. — (An I can read book)
    Newly illustrated ed.
    Summary: After Freddy is pushed into deep water by a couple
of toughs, he decides to learn to swim.
    ISBN 0-06-028484-6. — ISBN 0-06-028485-4 (lib. bdg.)
    ISBN 0-06-444262-4 (pbk.)
    [1. Swimming—Fiction.]   I. Title.   II. Series.
PZ7.K484Las   1999   98-50882
[E]—dc21   CIP
                                                                        AC

❖
Newly illustrated edition, 1999
www.harperchildrens.com

Last One In
is a
ROTTEN EGG

"What a hot day," said Bobby.

"It is too hot to play ball.

It is too hot to run.

It is too hot to ride a bike."

"It is too hot to do anything,"

said Willie.

5

"It is not too hot

to go swimming!" said Bobby.

"Yes! Let's go swimming!"

said Willie.

"I will go home

and ask my mother," said Bobby.

"Me too," said Willie.

"Meet you here in five minutes."

Both of their mothers said yes.
"Now don't forget to take
your swimming trunks, Willie,"
his mother joked.

On the way to the city pool

Bobby and Willie met Freddy.

He was sitting on the steps

of his house.

He looked hot.

8

"Hey Freddy!

We are going swimming.

Want to come too?"

"I will ask my mother,"

said Freddy.

"You may go swimming,"

said his mother.

"But remember that you are not

a deep-water swimmer yet.

Just stay in the shallow water."

"I will stay in the shallow water,"

said Freddy.

He ran out of the house.

"I can go!" he shouted.

"Great!" said Willie. "Let's go!"

When they got to the locker room,

they put on their swimming trunks.

They took a fast shower

and ran out to the pool.

12

"Hey fellows! NO RUNNING!"

yelled Tom the lifeguard.

"You know the rules."

They looked at the list of rules.

RULES OF THE POOL

1. No running or pushing.
2. No fooling around.
3. No food near the pool.
4. Stay out of water
   right after eating.
5. Girls must wear bathing caps.
6. No one in the pool
   when lifeguard is not on duty.
7. Look before you dive.
8. No swimming in front
   of diving board.
9. Only deep-water swimmers
   can swim in deep water.
10. Be careful—don't be sorry!

TOM
Lifeguard

"Okay," said Willie.

"Who is going in first?"

He dipped his foot into the water.

"Yikes, it's cold!" he yelled.

Bobby jumped into the deep water.

"Last one in is a rotten egg!"

he yelled.

"Not me," said Willie.

He jumped into the deep water.

"I guess I am the rotten egg,"

said Freddy.

"I cannot go in the deep water."

He walked down to the other end

of the pool and jumped

into the shallow water.

17

"Hey, look at me!

I am a whale,"

said Willie.

18

"Hey, look at me!

I am a submarine,"

said Bobby.

"Look at me!" yelled Willie.

"Look at this big splash."

"Want to see

a *really* big splash?"

yelled Bobby.

"That was good," said Freddy.

"I wish I could do that."

"Let's play tag," said Bobby.

"Freddy is *it*."

"Oh, that's not fair," said Freddy.

"I cannot swim in the deep water.

I will be *it* all day!"

"Okay," said Willie.

"We will do something else."

Two girls swam by.

"Do you boys want to race us?"

the girls asked.

"Oh, come on now," said Willie.

"We don't want to beat

you girls in a race."

"Yes," said Bobby. "We will win,

and then you will cry."

"No, we won't. Let's race!"

said the girls.

"Okay. You asked for it,"

said Bobby.

Freddy was the starter.

"Ready! *Get set!* GO!"

Willie swam fast.

Bobby swam fast.

But the two girls swam faster.

They beat the boys by three feet.

"Do you want to race again?"
asked the girls.
"Not today," said Willie.
"Bobby and I are too tired
from all that diving.
We will race you another day."

"Those girls are

really fast swimmers," said Willie.

"But we are better divers,"

said Bobby.

Freddy watched them dive.

He sat by the side of the pool

with his feet in the deep water.

"One day I will be

a good diver too,"

he said very softly.

Across the pool

two big boys

were fooling around.

They were pushing

the little kids into the water.

Suddenly the boys

came up behind Freddy.

"In you go!" they yelled.

They pushed him into the pool.

Freddy fell into the deep water.

Down,

down,

down he went.

He came up to the top.

Then he sank down, down again.

He opened his mouth

to yell for help.

But he only

swallowed more water.

He reached out—

and there was a hand grabbing his.

It was Tom the lifeguard.

Tom pulled Freddy out.

Freddy sat down on the bench.

He was full of water.

He coughed.

"What are you trying to do,

drink all the water in the pool?"

Tom made a little joke.

But it was no joke to Freddy.

He felt terrible.

36

He wanted to cry,

but he did not want Willie

or Bobby to see him cry.

He sat and shook.

He was cold.

As they walked home Bobby said,
"I just hope we find those two boys
who pushed Freddy into the pool."

"Let's go swimming again
tomorrow," said Willie.

"I will see how I feel," said Freddy.

The next day Bobby and Willie

stopped at Freddy's house.

"Let's go swimming," said Willie.

"I can't," said Freddy. "I am sick."

"What is the matter?"

asked Bobby.

"I have a bad cold," said Freddy.

"You don't look very sick,"

said Bobby.

"We will see you tomorrow.

Hope you feel better,"

said Willie.

The next day they were back again.

"How is your cold today?"

they asked.

"It's all better," said Freddy.

"Then let's go swimming,"

said Willie.

"I can't go swimming.

I hurt my leg," said Freddy.

Freddy's mother was looking

out of the window.

"Why don't you go swimming

with Willie and Bobby?"

she called.

"My leg hurts," said Freddy.

"I think the water

will make your leg

feel better," she said.

"And maybe you can learn

how to swim in the deep water.

I am sure that Tom will help you."

"Well, I will go," said Freddy,

"but I don't know

how I can swim

with my sore leg."

"Hi, Freddy," said Tom.

"It's good to see you back.

Now don't drink up all the water."

Freddy laughed.

"I want to learn to swim

in the deep water," he said.

"Can you teach me how?"

"Jump in," said Tom.

"Show me how you swim."

Freddy swam.

"You are splashing too much.

Easy does it.

Let's learn to swim

the right way," said Tom.

"First we will work on

your breathing.

Blow bubbles," said Tom.

Freddy did it.

"That is good," said Tom.

"Now let's learn how to float.

Don't worry," he said.

"I will not let you go under."

Soon Freddy could float

all by himself.

"Now I want you to kick like this:

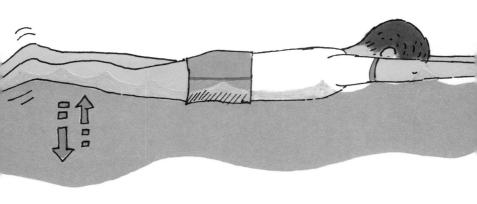

and move your arms like this:

You try it," said Tom.

Freddy did what Tom told him to do.

"That's a little better," said Tom.

"Work on these things every day,

and you will be in the deep water

very soon."

"You kick very well

for a boy with a sore leg,"

said Bobby.

"It is much better now,"

said Freddy. He smiled.

Freddy worked hard.

Every day he did this:

He learned how to tread water.

He kept getting better.

"Today let's try swimming
in the deep water," said Tom.
"Freddy is going to swim
in the deep water!"
yelled Bobby.
"Good boy, Freddy!
You will make it," said Willie.

Freddy jumped in.

He swam and swam and swam

to the other side of the pool.

"I did it! I did it!

I can swim in the deep water!"

"You are a good swimmer now,"

said Tom.

"Hey, let's swim," said Willie.

He jumped into the deep water.

"Look at me! I am a cannonball,"

he shouted.

"Look at me! I am a big fish,"

yelled Freddy.

"Hey, look over *there*!"

said Bobby.

"Those are the two guys

who pushed Freddy

into the pool."

The two boys were at it again.

They were pushing

the little kids into the pool.

Freddy got out of the pool.

"Hey, you two!" yelled Freddy.

"Just stop it."

"Are you talking to us?"

they asked.

"Yes," said Freddy. "Just stop

what you are doing."

They looked at Freddy and laughed.

"Are you going to stop us?"

"Yes, he is going to stop you,"
said Willie.

"He sure is," said Bobby.

"And *I* am going to stop you *too*!"

said Tom. "Get out

and do not come back

until you can follow the rules."

"Last one in is a rotten egg!"

said Freddy.

"Not me!" yelled Willie.

"Not me!" yelled Bobby.

They all jumped into the water
at the same time.

They all came up at the same time.

"Well," said Freddy.

"There are *no* rotten eggs here!"